Mark Zuckerberg and Facebook

Other titles in the *Technology Titans* series include:

Elon Musk and Tesla

Jeff Bezos and Amazon

Larry Page, Sergey Brin, and Google

Reed Hastings and Netflix

Steve Jobs and Apple

Mark Zuckerberg
and Facebook

Stuart A. Kallen

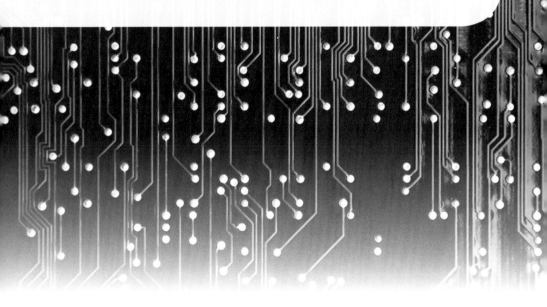

ReferencePoint Press®

San Diego, CA

© 2016 ReferencePoint Press, Inc.
Printed in the United States

For more information, contact:
ReferencePoint Press, Inc.
PO Box 27779
San Diego, CA 92198
www.ReferencePointPress.com

LIBRARY OF CONGRESS CATALOGING-IN-PUBLICATION DATA

Kallen, Stuart A., 1955-
  Mark Zuckerberg and facebook / by Stuart A. Kallen.
     pages cm. -- (Technology titans)
  Audience: Grade 9 to 12.
  Includes bibliographical references and index.
  ISBN-13: 978-1-60152-876-6 (hardback)
  ISBN-10: 1-60152-876-0 (hardback)
  1. Zuckerberg, Mark, 1984- 2. Facebook (Firm)--Juvenile literature. 3. Facebook (Electronic resource)--Juvenile literature. 4. Webmasters--United States--Biography--Juvenile literature.
  I. Title.
  HM479.Z83K35 2016
  006.7092--dc23
  [B]
                                                                        2015016551

Contents

The New Face of Tech

By the time Mark Zuckerberg celebrated his thirtieth birthday in 2015, he was one of the wealthiest and most successful tech titans in the world. As the founder of the social networking site Facebook, Zuckerberg gained his fame and fortune by fundamentally changing the way more than 1.4 billion people communicate and interact online.

Thanks to Facebook, Zuckerberg became one of the youngest billionaires in the United States when he was only twenty-three. Three years later, in 2010, Zuckerberg was named Person of the Year by *Time* magazine: "For connecting more than half a billion people and mapping the social relations among them, for creating a new system of exchanging information and for changing how we live our lives."[1]

Launched in a Dorm Room

Like many tech visionaries, Zuckerberg started small. He launched Facebook from his dorm room at Harvard University on February 4, 2004. The site, which was then only designed for use by Harvard students, was instantly popular. As news of Facebook spread to other campuses, Zuckerberg enlisted his dorm roommates to help him create exclusive Facebook websites for dozens of other colleges and universities nationwide. After Facebook membership was opened to the general public in 2006, the site's popularity exploded around the globe. In 2012 Facebook announced it had 1 billion users, and it was rated the second-most accessed site on the World Wide Web after the search engine Google.

Zuckerberg's rise to the top of the tech world began amid controversy. When he launched an early website called Facemash at Harvard in 2003, he illegally hacked into the university's computer network and posted private student photo ID images to the website. Zuckerberg could have been suspended for this breach. But he escaped serious punishment by volunteering to fix security flaws in Harvard's computer network. A year later, after Zuckerberg launched Facebook, he was sued by three Harvard seniors who accused him of stealing their idea for the site.

Even after its rather troubled beginnings, Facebook has regularly come under fire from users concerned about privacy and marketing issues. For example, it was revealed in 2013 that Facebook kept a running log of websites visited by users whether they were logged into the service or not. This allowed advertisers to target ads based on a user's private web-browsing habits.

Worldwide Facebook

Controversies have not affected Facebook's popularity. In 2015 about one in every five people on earth had a Facebook account. And few can deny Zuckerberg's achievements. As *Time* correspondent Lev Grossman described it in the Person of the Year article, "Zuckerberg wired together a twelfth of humanity into a single network, thereby creating a social entity almost twice as large as the US. If Facebook were a country, it would be the third largest, behind only China and India."[2]

> "Zuckerberg wired together a twelfth of humanity into a single network, thereby creating a social entity almost twice as large as the US."[2]
>
> —Lev Grossman, *Time* correspondent.

Furthermore, Zuckerberg thinks of Facebook as only the first step in a farsighted plan. As he said in 2014, "Our goal . . . is to make affordable access to basic Internet services available to every person in the world."[3] To make that a reality, Zuckerberg launched an initiative called the Connectivity Lab, which is examining ways to use solar-powered drones and futuristic lasers to provide Internet access to remote areas. Additionally, in 2014 Zuckerberg purchased the virtual reality headset maker Oculus VR. He sees long-term applications for virtual reality technology in communications, entertainment, and more.

Giving It Away

Zuckerberg has a well-defined vision of Facebook's future, but he often makes it clear he is not motivated by money. His Facebook salary is a

Facebook founder Mark Zuckerberg visits Harvard University, where Facebook was launched. In 2015, one in five people worldwide possessed a Facebook account.

symbolic one dollar a year, and he regularly wears jeans, hoodies, and rubber sandals to work. Unlike most billionaires who buy exotic sports cars, Zuckerberg was driving a $30,000 Volkswagen GTI with a manual transmission in 2015.

Even if Zuckerberg seems not to have changed due to Facebook's success, what began as his dorm-room project has transformed the world. Facebook activities such as posting photos, commenting, and "liking" posts have become commonplace in modern society. In less than a decade, the site changed the way many people stay in touch, how they consume news and media content, and the way they think about sharing the most intimate details of their lives. As for Facebook's founder, he has been called brilliant, self-confident, and single-minded, and he has even been labeled an evil genius. Whatever the case, as a young man with great plans, Zuckerberg is only at the beginning of his project to connect humanity to the Internet and people to one another.

> "Our goal . . . is to make affordable access to basic Internet services available to every person in the world."[3]
>
> —Mark Zuckerberg, Facebook founder.

Chapter 1

A Computer Prodigy

Mark Elliot Zuckerberg was born on May 14, 1984, in Dobbs Ferry, New York. Mark's father, Edward, was a dentist known as "Painless Dr. Z." He specialized in treating patients who were afraid of going to the dentist; Dr. Z's motto was "We cater to cowards."[4] Zuckerberg's mother, Karen, was originally a psychiatrist, but she quit her job to raise her children and manage her husband's dental practice. Edward calls Karen "my most overqualified employee."[5]

Edward grew up in the Flatbush neighborhood of Brooklyn, New York. He excelled in math and science and wanted to work with computers However, in the early 1970s, before the advent of personal computers, studying computer science did not seem practical. As Edward explains:

> Growing up Jewish in New York City, if you had half a brain, your parents wanted you to be a doctor or a dentist. I was actually a numbers guy. But back then, there really weren't a lot of jobs in computer programming. There were these big, room-size computers that you read about. . . . That was not the "appropriate use of my time," my parents would have said. It wasn't for the smart boys.[6]

Giving in to his parent's wishes, Edward went to dental college in 1975. He and Karen were married in 1979, and a year later they bought a big house in Dobbs Ferry, a small, affluent village in Westchester County, 25 miles (40 km) north of New York City. For years, Edward commuted between his dental practice in Brooklyn and his home in Dobbs Ferry.

A Strong-Willed Child

In 1982 the Zuckerbergs had their first child, a daughter named Randi. Mark was the second child and has two younger sisters. Donna was born in 1987, and Arielle was born in 1989. The year Donna came along, Edward moved the dental practice from Brooklyn to the basement of his Dobbs Ferry home. He loved deep-sea diving, so he decorated his office with aquatic knickknacks like seashells and fishnets. A huge, 200-gallon (757 L) fish tank dominated one wall in the operating room.

According to Edward, working at home with Karen created a perfect environment for raising a family. "My wife was a superwoman," he once commented. "She managed to work and be home. We had a unique situation because my office was in the house. I highly recommend it if it works for your occupation. It did afford the ability to work and be home with the kids at the same time."[7]

> "Growing up Jewish in New York City, if you had half a brain, your parents wanted you to be a doctor or a dentist. I was actually a numbers guy. But back then, there really weren't a lot of jobs in computer programming."[6]
>
> —Edward Zuckerberg, father of Mark Zuckerberg.

The situation also meant the family had first-rate dental care. To this day, Mark claims he has no dental cavities, thanks to his father's profession. But even when they were not getting free dental work, the Zuckerberg kids would wander in and out of Edward's basement office. According to his father, Mark often wanted to play with the dental tools and machines, which sparked his interest in technology. And, as Edward states, when Mark wanted something, he was strong-willed and often got his way:

For some kids, their questions could be answered with a simple yes or no. For Mark, if he asked for something, yes by itself would work, but no required much more. If you were going to say no to him, you had better be prepared with a strong argument backed by facts, experiences, logic, reasons. We envisioned him becoming a lawyer one day, with a near 100% success rate of convincing juries.[8]

The Zuckerberg family surrounds Mark (seated) in a family portrait. From left to right are Zuckerberg's older sister, Randi; father, Edward; mother, Karen; and younger sister Arielle. A third sister, Donna, is not pictured. The family lived in Dobbs Ferry, New York, during Mark's childhood years.

Building Games

In addition to dental machines, Edward had numerous computers in the home. In 1978 he purchased an early model personal computer called an Atari 800. The 10-pound (4.5 kg) cream-colored machine looked like an old-fashioned electric typewriter and had less memory than a modern coffeemaker. But the Atari could be programmed to perform simple tasks. Edward used it with a custom dial-up modem provided by his bank to make mortgage payments electronically. He was so amazed by this process, he told Karen that computers would revolutionize modern society. She scoffed, pointing out that she could write three checks in three minutes while it took him an hour of programming to get the primitive Atari to make a single payment. Edward later recalled that due to its limited applications, the machine was "awful," but he had few regrets about buying it: "My lesson learned was not to be afraid to dabble in technology early. Not to be one of those guys stuck waiting."[9]

Edward moved on to bigger and faster computers, but the Atari 800 would play an important role in the Facebook story. When Mark was six years old, his father taught him to write computer code for the Atari. According to Edward, he bought Mark a book called *Atari BASIC Programming*, but "ultimately his ability to program was self-taught."[10]

Compared to other home computers available at the time, such as the Apple II and the Commodore PET, the Atari 800 offered advanced graphics and sound capabilities. This made the machine perfect for Mark, who loved playing the early computer game *Star Raiders*. Released in 1979, *Star Raiders* was a space combat simulator video game that allowed users to fight off an invading fleet of alien Zylon spaceships.

"If you were going to say no to [Mark], you had better be prepared with a strong argument backed by facts, experiences, logic, reasons. We envisioned him becoming a lawyer one day."[8]

—Edward Zuckerberg, father of Mark Zuckerberg.

By the time Mark was ten in 1994, Edward had a much better computer, a Quantex 486DX, which ran Windows 3.1. And Mark used the machine to become an expert coder. While some kids were playing computer games, Zuckerberg was creating them. As he later recalled, "I had a bunch of friends who were artists. They'd come over, draw stuff, and I'd build a game out of it."[11]

Excelling in Computers

Edward wanted to support Mark's programming talents, so he hired software developer David Newman as a tutor. According to Newman, the twelve-year-old Zuckerberg "was a prodigy. Sometimes it was tough to stay ahead of him."[12] Newman eventually lost track of his pupil in later years and was stunned to find out in 2010 that Zuckerberg had created Facebook.

After working a short time with Newman, Zuckerberg enrolled in a Thursday-night graduate computer course at nearby Mercy College. When Dr. Zuckerberg dropped preteen Mark off for the first class, the instructor pointed to the short, skinny kid and told Edward, "You can't bring him into the classroom with you."[13] Edward told the instructor that it was not he but his son who was the student.

Pinging on ZuckNet

The computers in the Zuckerberg household increased in number as Edward became one of the first dentists to use the machines for digital radiography. Instead of using traditional photographic film to take dental X-rays, digital radiography employs digital sensors, which create X-ray imagery. Edward also had business computers for his dentist office, and Mark and his sisters each had their own machines.

When Mark was twelve, he used the computers to solve a problem in the large Zuckerberg home. There was no intercom, so the family and dental staff communicated by shouting. For example, when a dental patient showed up at the front door, their arrival was announced by someone upstairs yelling to the receptionist down in the basement. To improve household communications, Mark created a messaging software program he called ZuckNet, which linked all the computers in the house.

ZuckNet sent messages by a method called pinging. Ping was a basic Internet program that allowed a user to verify that an individual Internet address existed and could accept messages. It made a pinging sound when a message was received. Dr. Zuckerberg's computer announced when a patient arrived, and the children communicated with each other from their bedroom computers. ZuckNet was a primitive version of America Online (AOL) Instant Messenger, which came out the following year.

As his interest in coding grew, Zuckerberg began reading complicated books about programming. The first was *C++ for Dummies*, which

Encourage Their Passions

In a 2012 profile in *New York* magazine, Edward Zuckerberg was asked how a mild-mannered dentist had managed to raise the billionaire founder of Facebook. Edward answered:

> Look, you have successful kids, and people are going to want to emulate your formula. But we don't profess any special child-rearing skills. The best I can say is that as parents, you can engineer the life you want your kids to have, but it may not be the life they want to have. You have to encourage them to pursue their passions. And you have to spend more time on them than you spend on anything else.

Quoted in Matthew Shaer, "The Zuckerbergs of Dobbs Ferry," *New York*, May 6, 2012. http://nymag.com.

covered the complex topic of object-oriented programming. This sort of coding manipulates units of data, or objects, and organizes them to perform various tasks. Examples of objects include scroll bars on a computer desktop and shopping cart buttons on a commercial website. Although *C++ for Dummies* was written for experienced computer programmers, Zuckerberg devoured the content while still in middle school.

Fun with the Family

Like many other tech lovers, Zuckerberg was a huge fan of the futuristic *Star Wars* films. When he was eleven, Zuckerberg enlisted his sisters to film a parody of the movies called *The Star Wars Sill-ogy*. Although the movie was supposed to be funny, the Zuckerberg kids took their jobs very seriously. They held production meetings every morning, built sets, and created costumes. Mark played Luke Skywalker, the central protagonist in the film. Since his voice had not yet changed with the onset of puberty, Mark spoke in a high, squeaky voice. Two-year-old Arielle played the robot R2-D2, wearing a garbage can over her head. Zuckerberg's love of

A poster advertises the 1977 movie Star Wars, the first in the popular futuristic series. As a child, Zuckerberg was an avid fan of the films, even playing the role of Luke Skywalker (center) in a film parody that he created with his sisters.

Star Wars continued for many years. When he was thirteen he had a bar mitzvah, a Jewish ceremony in which a boy is initiated into adulthood. Zuckerberg's bar mitzvah party had a *Star Wars* theme.

Zuckerberg also loved to play practical jokes. One night he used ZuckNet to scare his sister Donna. She was working on her computer when a message popped up on the screen saying the device was infected with a deadly virus and would blow up in thirty seconds. As the machine counted down to zero, Donna ran out of the room screaming.

Mark also planned a practical joke for New Year's Eve 1999, based on his parent's fears of what was called the Year 2000 problem, or Y2K bug. In the late 1990s there was widespread concern over the way computer dates were abbreviated; to save space on computer memory chips, only the last two digits of the year were used. The Y2K problem was based on the theory that the programming bug would cause computers to register the date as 1900 when the year turned over to 2000. Some believed this glitch would cause banks to lose their financial records, airplanes to crash, and nuclear power plants to melt down. Some people stocked up on food, water, toilet paper, and even guns in anticipation of a Y2K disaster.

Zuckerberg's parents did not arm themselves, but they were concerned about the Y2K bug. Knowing this, Zuckerberg waited until exactly midnight on December 31. When the date rolled over to January 1, 2000, he shut off the electrical power in the house at the circuit breaker in the basement. After frightening his family, Zuckerberg switched the power back on, giving everyone a laugh. As for the Y2K bug, most computers were fixed in anticipation of the new year, and few problems were encountered.

"Controlled Yet Sometimes Undisciplined"
Zuckerberg attended Ardsley High School in Ardsley, New York, in ninth and tenth grade. At Ardsley, Zuckerberg's studies in Latin led him to invent a digital version of the board game Risk, set in the Roman Empire. The computer game featured a virtual general called Julius Caesar who was so skilled at military strategy even Zuckerberg had trouble defeating him. However, Zuckerberg felt that Ardsley did not offer enough high-level computer science and math courses for him to continually improve his programming skills. In 2000, in search of a better education for their son, the Zuckerbergs enrolled Mark in Phillips Exeter Academy, a prestigious prep school.

Zuckerberg was a voracious reader. At the academy he excelled at languages, later saying he learned to read and write French, Hebrew, Latin, and ancient Greek. He was known to recite lines from epic Greek poems such as *The Iliad*, written by the author Homer around 1250 BCE. At Exeter, Zuckerberg earned a diploma in classical studies and won academic prizes in astronomy, math, and physics.

Although computers remained central to his life, Zuckerberg had other interests. He joined the fencing team and soon became captain. He was later named the team's most valuable player. Zuckerberg described his love for fencing on his enrollment application to Harvard University. When answering a question about his most meaningful activity, he wrote, "Amidst a hectic week of work, fencing has always proven to be the perfect medium; for it is both social and sport, mental and athletic, and controlled yet sometimes undisciplined."[14] Five years later, as the popularity of Facebook was increasing, Harvard writing teacher Elizabeth L. Greenspan analyzed the essay answer: "Zuckerberg seems to be offering up 'fencing' as a [symbol] for himself, that Zuckerberg is—or imagines himself to be—both social and sport, mental and athletic, and controlled yet sometimes undisciplined."[15]

> "Amidst a hectic week of work, fencing has always proven to be the perfect medium; for it is both social and sport, mental and athletic, and controlled yet sometimes undisciplined."[14]
>
> —Mark Zuckerberg, Facebook founder.

A Million-Dollar Idea

Whatever the psychology behind Zuckerberg's essay, Harvard accepted his application. But first he had to finish his last year of high school at Exeter. As a senior in 2002, Zuckerberg was required to submit a final project for graduation that would be graded on quality and originality. However, Zuckerberg did not have any project ideas. While he was discussing this problem with his friend Adam D'Angelo, the MP3 music player on his computer played the last song in his playlist and stopped. Zuckerberg felt the MP3 player should know what he wanted to hear next and continue playing. Thus, a school project idea was born.

Two fencers compete. At Phillips Exeter Academy, Zuckerberg excelled in fencing, becoming captain of the team. He went on to describe the sport as his most meaningful activity on his application to Harvard University.

Zuckerberg and D'Angelo (who later became Facebook's chief technical officer) designed the Synapse Media Player. Synapse had features commonly seen today on Pandora and other music apps, but it was quite advanced for the time. The player used artificial intelligence to learn a user's listening habits, recommend music, and create playlists based on the listener's tastes.

The Synapse project received a good grade at Exeter, and Zuckerberg posted a free version of the player on the Internet under the company name Intelligent Media Group. Synapse was reviewed by *PC Magazine*, which gave it a rating of 3 out of 5. The player also got a good review from the tech website Slashdot. The Synapse app became popular when tech bloggers began writing about it, prompting Microsoft and AOL to

Zuckerberg the Hacker

Mark Zuckerberg admits that he is a hacker and has been one since he created his family's communication software ZuckNet in 1995. Zuckerberg believes that hacker culture, or what he calls the Hacker Way, is about sharing effort and knowledge. He is convinced hackers can produce great things that are better than something an individual can do alone. What follows is a 2012 letter Zuckerberg wrote to company investors in which he explained the Hacker Way:

> The word "hacker" has an unfairly negative connotation from being portrayed in the media as people who break into computers. In reality, hacking just means building something quickly or testing the boundaries of what can be done. Like most things, it can be used for good or bad, but the vast majority of hackers I've met tend to be idealistic people who want to have a positive impact on the world. . . .
>
> Hackers believe that something can always be better, and that nothing is ever complete. They just have to go fix it—often in the face of people who say it's impossible. . . . Hacking is also an inherently hands-on and active discipline. Instead of debating for days whether a new idea is possible or what the best way to build something is, hackers would rather just prototype something and see what works. . . . Hackers believe that the best idea and implementation should always win—not the person who is best at lobbying for an idea or the person who manages the most people.

Mark Zuckerberg, "Mark Zuckerberg's Letter to Investors: 'The Hacker Way,'" *Wired*, February 2, 2012. www.wired.com.

make bids for the software. As Zuckerberg tells it, "One of the companies offered us $950,000 but wanted us to go work for them for 3 years. We wanted to go to college, so we said no."[16]

As a dedicated computer hacker, Zuckerberg had another reason for turning down nearly $1 million. Like many hackers, he strongly believed that a good piece of software should not be owned by a single company.

Zuckerberg stated, "It's important to us that people are able to use the software for free. Software belongs to everyone. No matter what kind of deal we get into, we're going to try to keep it free."[17]

Code Monkey

After graduating from Exeter in 2002, Zuckerberg began attending his courses at Harvard. Tech journalist David Kirkpatrick describes him at that time: "Mark Zuckerberg was a short, slender, intense introvert [shy person] with curly brown

hair whose fresh freckled face made him look closer to fifteen than the nineteen he was. His uniform was baggy jeans, rubber sandals—even in winter—and a T-shirt that usually had some sort of clever picture or phrase."[18] One of Zuckerberg's favorite T-shirts slogans read "Code Monkey," a reference to his love of writing computer code.

Like other code monkeys, Zuckerberg was more interested in programming than carrying on a conversation. When others were talking, he often remained quiet and said nothing until the others were done. But Zuckerberg's mind was working even as his mouth stayed shut. Kirkpatrick explains:

> He stared. He would stare at you while you were talking, and stay absolutely silent. If you said something stimulating, he'd finally fire up his own ideas and the words would come cascading out. But if you went on too long or said something obvious, he would start looking through you. When you finished, he'd quietly mutter "yeah," then change the subject or turn away.[19]

Zuckerberg opened up around women, and his confidence, sly smile, and sense of humor attracted his future wife, Priscilla Chan. She was a student at Harvard who had been voted "class genius" when she attended high school in Boston. The two met at a party at Alpha Epsilon Pi, a fraternity for Jewish students where Zuckerberg was a member.

By his sophomore year at Harvard, Zuckerberg had a reputation as a premier software developer. However, his major was not computer science but psychology. Zuckerberg later explained he chose to make psychology his focus so he could help people achieve happiness. "I just think people are the most interesting thing—other people," he said. "What it comes down to, for me, is that people want to do what will make them happy, but in order to [achieve] that they really have to understand their world and what is going on around them."[20]

A Tight-Knit Family

Zuckerberg's pursuit of understanding what makes people happy helped make him a world-famous CEO. However, even though Mark's fame and fortune have placed demands on his time, he still remains tightly connected to his family. They now all live in the San Francisco Bay Area and regularly visit one another. And Mark is not the only well-known Zuckerberg. Randi went to work for her brother in 2005 as Facebook's head of consumer marketing and social-good initiatives. In 2014 she launched her own media company, Dot Complicated, a digital lifestyle website. Randi also appeared on a Bravo TV reality show on Silicon Valley entrepreneurs.

Donna Zuckerberg received a PhD in classics from Princeton University and is a baker, writer, and photographer who runs Sugar Mountain Treats, a food website. In 2014 Arielle launched Humin, a smartphone app designed to manage phone numbers and contacts. When announcing the phone app, Arielle was asked why she never worked at Facebook. She replied, "Who wants to work for their older brother?"[21]

Of course none of the Zuckerbergs have to work, thanks to Mark's genius. Urged on by his father, he was performing tasks on a computer as a first grader that many adults could barely comprehend. Zuckerberg wrote countless lines of code to help his family communicate better, and he devised a music player that attracted the attention of the biggest names in tech. Those at Harvard who knew Zuck, as he is still called, expected him to be successful. However, few could imagine what lay ahead for the self-proclaimed code monkey from Dobbs Ferry, New York.

Chapter 2

From Facemash to Thefacebook

When nineteen-year-old Mark Zuckerberg began his sophomore year at Harvard University in September 2003, he took classes in psychology, art history, and computer science, but most of his time was spent hacking. Zuckerberg kept an 8-foot-long (2.4 m) whiteboard in the hall outside his four-person room at Harvard's Kirkland House dormitory—the whiteboard was too big to fit inside the small room. Zuckerberg scribbled out concepts and formulas on the whiteboard; many of the notions were for new Internet services. As his dorm roommate Dustin Moskovitz recalls, "He really loved that whiteboard. He always wanted to draw out his ideas, even when that didn't necessarily make them clearer."[22]

Dorm Life

Since Zuckerberg's dorm room was very small, he spent much of his time in the Kirkland House common room hunched over his PC. When creating code, Zuckerberg slept little and rarely took time to eat properly. His desk in the common room was littered with empty energy drink bottles, soda cans, and crumpled fast-food wrappers.

Zuckerberg and Moskovitz shared their dorm room with Chris Hughes, a literature and history major, and Billy Olson, who was interested in acting. The room had bunk beds, but they were dismantled and placed side-by-side in an effort to maintain fairness; this way no one would have to sleep on the upper bunk. There was hardly room to move; the beds took up most of the space, and the desks were piled high with computers, electronic gadgets, wires, and trash.

Chris Hughes (right) is pictured with Zuckerberg at Harvard University, where the two were roommates. Although Hughes had little interest in the Internet before rooming with Zuckerberg, he went on to become a cocreator of Facebook.

Although the space was cramped, the four students got along with one another despite Zuckerberg's tendency to be blunt and painfully honest. One common bond the dorm mates shared was their interest in the Internet. Although Moskovitz was an economics major with little training in computer science, he provided a fresh way of looking at the web. He often engaged Zuckerberg in long conversations about various websites and which features made them good or bad. The two also discussed how the web might be used to change and improve the entire world.

Hughes and Olson started the year with little interest in the Internet, but living with Zuckerberg and Moskovitz changed their attitudes. They too were drawn into discussions and added their thoughts. Zuckerberg was a natural leader, and whenever he came up with an idea for a website, all three roommates would offer their opinions on how to make it of the highest quality.

Match and Mash

One of the first projects to emerge from Zuckerberg's dorm room at Kirkland House was an app called Course Match. The software program gave students the opportunity to view a list of all the other students taking a particular course. After assembling the site from information publicly posted on Harvard's website, Zuckerberg sent out e-mails about Course Match to his friends. Users spread the word to others, and the popularity of Course Match spread like a virus. The app was particularly popular with students who wanted to get close to potential dating partners by taking the same classes.

The success of Course Match inspired Zuckerberg to build on the idea using the theme of a popular website called Hot or Not. This site allowed users to rate the attractiveness of others who submitted their photos. Combining his code monkey skills with his offbeat sense of humor, Zuckerberg created Facemash, which invited users to compare the faces of two different people of the same sex and asked if they were "hot or not." As a person's hotness ratings increased, his or her picture would rise through the ranks and be compared to other attractive students.

Hacking Facebooks

Zuckerberg gathered the pictures on Facemash from what were called "facebooks." These were private websites maintained by each of Harvard's twelve undergrad dorms. They contained pictures of students taken the day they arrived for orientation. Most of the poses revealed awkward, slightly frightened students on their first day of college. Few of the students would have cared to share their facebook pictures with the world.

In the week before the launch of Facemash, Zuckerberg obtained the facebook pictures by various means. At Lowell House, a friend gave Zuckerberg a temporary password, which allowed Zuckerberg to log in to the dorm's computer system. (The friend later expressed regret.) At another house, Zuckerberg sneaked in and plugged his computer into the Ethernet cable in the wall. This allowed him to access the dorm's computer files and download names and pictures of the residents. David Kirkpatrick analyzed Zuckerberg's behavior: "The fact that he was doing something slightly illicit gave Zuckerberg little pause. He could be a touch headstrong and liked to stir things up. He didn't ask permission before proceeding. It's not that he sets out to break the rules; he just doesn't pay much attention to them."[23]

> "It's not that [Zuckerberg] sets out to break the rules; he just doesn't pay much attention to them."[23]
>
> —David Kirkpatrick, tech journalist.

The home page for Facemash posed two questions and answers: "Were we let in [to Harvard] for our looks? No. Will we be judged by them? Yes."[24] Zuckerberg's brutal honesty was further displayed in a journal that he posted on the Facemash website. The journal was written as Zuckerberg was creating Facemash, and in it he admits he was a little intoxicated during its inception. He writes that he was upset with a girl who rejected him and calls her an offensive name. He added, "Some of these people have pretty horrendous facebook pics. I almost want to put some of these faces next to pictures of farm animals and have people vote on which is more attractive."[25]

Not So Hot

Zuckerberg used his laptop computer to launch Facemash at 7:00 a.m. October 31, 2003. He initially e-mailed the website address to a few friends. Although Zuckerberg said he only wanted people to test the site, the testers forwarded the link to their own friends, and the site went viral. By the time Zuckerberg returned to his dorm room at 10:00 p.m., his laptop was overloaded by 450 Facemash users who by this time had compared twenty-two thousand pairs of photos. Unable to use his computer, Zuckerberg pulled the plug on Facemash at 10:30 p.m.

The Social Network

Mark Zuckerberg's years at Harvard University and his founding of Facebook were detailed in director David Fincher's 2010 movie *The Social Network*, starring Jesse Eisenberg. The film is based on the 2009 Ben Mezrich book *The Accidental Billionaires: The Founding of Facebook; A Tale of Sex, Money, Genius, and Betrayal.*

The Social Network portrays Zuckerberg as both a genius and an angry, socially inept individual desperate to impress the Harvard elite while searching for a girlfriend. Although *The Social Network* received widespread acclaim and eight Academy Award nominations, Zuckerberg said the movie was an inaccurate portrayal of his life. Contrary to the message of the film, Zuckerberg said he was not interested in joining Harvard's social clubs. Additionally, he did not create Facebook to impress girls; he was already dating his future wife, Priscilla Chan, at the time. However, Zuckerberg did admit *The Social Network* got his wardrobe right, as he later told an audience at Stanford University: "It's interesting the stuff that they focused on getting right—like every single shirt and fleece they had in that movie is actually a shirt or fleece that I own."

Quoted in Ben Child, "Mark Zuckerberg Rejects His Portrayal in 'The Social Network,'" *Guardian* (Manchester), October 20, 2010. www.theguardian.com.

Within days the staff of the *Harvard Crimson*, the university newspaper, issued an editorial criticizing Zuckerberg for bringing out the worst in Harvard students by encouraging them to judge one another on the basis of their looks. The editorial called Zuckerberg's facebook hacks "guerrilla computing"[26] and said the site would not have been so bad if people had given permission for their pictures to be used. But even as the *Crimson* scolded Zuckerberg, it described the appeal of the site:

Students could log onto an open website and compare . . . the better-looking of an infinite, randomly-generated sequence of paired mugs. A peculiarly-squinting senior and that hottie from your Medieval manuscripts section—click! Your [dorm] mate and the kid who always glared at you in Annenberg [dining hall]—click! Your two best friends' respective significant others—pause . . . click, click, click! . . . We Harvard students could indulge our fondness for judging those around us on superficial criteria without ever having to face any of the judged in person.[27]

An Apology

The creator of Facemash was forced to face a judgment of his own. On November 18 Zuckerberg was called before Harvard's disciplinary administrative board. He was charged with breaching security, violating copyrights, and violating individual privacy. Although he could have been expelled from Harvard, he was put on probation and required to see a counselor.

After the Facemash fiasco, Zuckerberg was quick to apologize in an e-mail to the *Crimson*, saying he did not intend the site to be seen by so many people: "I hope you understand, this is not how I meant for things to go, and I apologize for any harm done as a result of my neglect to consider how quickly the site would spread and its consequences thereafter. . . . I definitely see how my intentions could be seen in the wrong light."[28]

Although Zuckerberg said he was sorry, he celebrated his light punishment with a bottle of very expensive champagne. And some saw Zuckerberg as a hero; he had created a website that people found instantly addictive.

Connecting People

Although Facemash was dead, Zuckerberg continued to create websites meant to link people through mutual references, meaning shared interests and experiences. "I had this hobby of just building these little projects," he said. "I had like twelve projects that year. Of course I wasn't fully committed to any one of them. [Most of them were about] seeing how people were connected through mutual references."[29]

One of Zuckerberg's projects linked students who were in one of his classes, Art in the Time of Augustus. Augustus was a Roman emperor who came to power in 27 BCE, and the class required students to memorize data about more than two hundred pieces of art from that era. Zuckerberg rarely attended the class, and when it was almost time to take the final exam, he needed a way to learn the course material fast.

He hacked together a website that featured hundreds of art images from class. The site provided a space where users could write the historical significance of each piece. As Zuckerberg recalls, "I emailed this to the class list and said, 'Hey guys, I built this study tool.'"[30] Within two hours, all of the images had numerous notes added by individual students. Zuckerberg was able to study the notes created by others and pass the test. As he later said, "I did very well in that class. We all did."[31]

> "I had this hobby of just building these little projects. I had like twelve projects that year [2003]. . . . [Most of them were about] seeing how people were connected."[29]
>
> —Mark Zuckerberg, Facebook founder.

Still fascinated by the idea of connecting people, Zuckerberg took on a project conceived by three fans of the Facemash site. Divya Narendra was a mathematician, and Cameron and Tyler Winklevoss were 6-foot-5-inch identical twins who were champion rowers on the Harvard rowing team. The three students were interested in creating a dating and social networking website called the Harvard Connection, which later was renamed ConnectU. The site was meant to provide students with information about upcoming parties and offer discount coupons to local nightclubs. But Narendra and the Winklevoss brothers were not programmers, so they offered to pay Zuckerberg $400 to write code for their site. However, Zuckerberg later claimed he only did a minimal amount of work on the Harvard Connection because it would have required far more of his time than he was willing to commit.

Friendster and Thefacebook

Zuckerberg's link to Harvard Connection would later become the focus of a lawsuit. It was initiated by Narendra and the Winklevosses, who accused Zuckerberg of stealing their idea to create Facebook. The episode was also depicted in a popular 2010 film, *The Social Network*. But at the time, the Harvard Connection seemed to be imitating another social networking site that was exploding in popularity. The California-based Friendster was conceived as an informal dating website that allowed users to expand their list of possible romantic contacts. Users were encouraged to create their own individual profiles with photos, videos, and personal information such as date of birth, hometown, hobbies, and favorite music.

By late 2003 Friendster was nearly two years old and had more than 3 million users. But because the site was so popular, its computer servers were often overloaded. This caused Friendster pages to load very slowly,

Before Facebook, social networking sites such as Friendster were wildly popular among college students. Connectivity was sometimes slow, however—a problem Zuckerberg sought to overcome when creating his own social network.

and sometimes the site crashed completely. As a result, many Friendster users stopped visiting the site.

Whatever its technical difficulties, Friendster created momentum among Harvard students to use its facebooks to create a social network for the school. The *Crimson* organized the call for a campus-wide facebook and published an editorial in December 2003 called "Put Online a Happy Face: Electronic Facebook for the Entire College Should Be Both Helpful and Entertaining for All." The *Crimson* staff wrote:

> "A centralized facebook that includes the entire Harvard community . . . would allow easy access to the names of people that we all interact with daily."[32]
>
> —*Harvard Crimson* staff.

> The potential benefits of a comprehensive, campus-wide online facebook are plenty. A centralized facebook that includes the entire Harvard community . . . would allow easy access to the names of people that we all interact with daily. . . . Whether one is simply scoping an elusive classmate, or curious of a friend's first-year registration day photo—we all know the lure of that peculiar form of entertainment—a campus-wide facebook will facilitate the Harvard community with the names and basics of their peers, without worry of opening the site to unsolicited strangers.[32]

Eliminating Problems

The *Crimson* editorial listed several issues associated with creating an official Harvard online facebook. There were legal matters involved with posting private photos and information online. Therefore, the site would only be open to Harvard students. Individuals would have the right to opt out of the service or to have only preapproved portions of their profiles listed.

Aware of the buzz on campus, Zuckerberg believed a different approach could solve the issues. He wanted to let students upload whatever information they wanted to be made public. He later admitted that this idea was inspired by an earlier *Crimson* editorial, which stated, "Much of the trouble

Using Thefacebook

When Mark Zuckerberg launched Thefacebook at Harvard in February 2004, the site incorporated features that are familiar to today's Facebook users. As David Kirkpatrick explains, the site was also tailored to fit the needs of the students who used it:

> Much activity on Thefacebook from the beginning was driven by the [dating desires] of young adults. It asked you whether you were "interested in" men or women. In addition to giving you the option to list whether you were in a relationship, you were asked to fill in a section labeled "Looking for."
>
> Many people, on the other hand, found practical and wholesome uses for Thefacebook—creating study groups for classes, arranging meetings for clubs, and posting notices about parties. Thefacebook was a tool for self-expression, and even at this [early] stage of its development people were starting to recognize that there were many facets of the self that could be projected on its screen.
>
> Another feature was timely for many students. You could click on a course and see who was taking it. . . . At Thefacebook's launch, students were in the middle of choosing courses for the following semester. It was what's called "shopping week" at Harvard, when classes have begun but students can add or drop them at will. For any Harvard student who picked his or her courses partly based on who else was in class, this feature of Thefacebook was immediately useful. It helps explain the rapid spread of Thefacebook in its early days.

David Kirkpatrick, *The Facebook Effect*. New York: Simon & Schuster, 2010, p. 32.

surrounding the Facemash could have been eliminated if only the site had limited itself to students who voluntarily uploaded their own photos."[33]

On January 11, 2004, exactly one month after the *Crimson* editorial ran, Zuckerberg took an action that showed he was interested in creating his own version of a facebook for Harvard; he paid thirty-five dollars to register the website address Thefacebook.com. Inspired by the editorial and the popularity of Friendster and his own creations, Course Match and Facemash, Zuckerberg was hard at work building a website on which Harvard users could post information they were willing to share.

Because he knew the site would be at least as popular as Facemash, he had to acquire server space outside the university that could handle the number of users. Not hosting the site on Harvard's computer network also freed him from the worry that the school could influence or shut down his new enterprise. Zuckerberg paid eighty-five dollars a month to a network hosting company called Manage.com. This move allowed him to upload Thefacebook.com software and data to the Manage.com network, which had powerful servers to handle thousands of users and few restrictions on their use.

A Visualization of Your Social Network

Zuckerberg felt he had a great idea with Thefacebook but did not think he could undertake the project by himself. He enlisted Eduardo Saverin, who also belonged to his fraternity, Alpha Epsilon Pi. Saverin, the son of a wealthy Brazilian magazine publisher, was a master chess player, an officer of Harvard's Investment Club, and a business and math wizard. Zuckerberg offered Saverin one-third ownership in Thefacebook in exchange for a $1,000 investment and the promise to help popularize the website. Saverin accepted the terms.

On February 4, 2004, Thefacebook went live with a home page that explained: "Thefacebook is an online directory that connects people through social networks at colleges. We have opened up Thefacebook for popular consumption at Harvard University. You can use Thefacebook to: Search for people at your school; Find out who are in your classes; Look up your friends' friends; See a visualization of your social network."[34]

After opening three accounts for testing, Zuckerberg became Thefacebook user number four. Roommates Hughes and Moskovitz were users number five and six, and Saverin was user number seven. Zuckerberg and his friends e-mailed invites to Thefacebook to students at Kirkland House. These people sent out e-mails asking their network of friends to join, and Thefacebook went viral even faster than Facemash.

Four days after it was launched, Thefacebook had 650 registered members; the next day 300 more joined. By then students were talking about Thefacebook in hallways, dorm rooms, and the dining halls. Some could barely stop updating their profiles long enough to attend class.

Thefacebook had many features similar to today's Facebook. Students uploaded a profile picture and stated their relationship status, e-mail address, phone number, and favorite books, movies, and music. Users could also list the courses they were taking and their political affiliations, choosing between very liberal, liberal, moderate, conservative, very conservative, and apathetic. There was even the option to "poke" somebody, or get their attention with a poke icon that appeared on their Facebook page. Zuckerberg provided no content, photos, or statements; Thefacebook was a software platform on which users created their own content.

Like today's Facebook, the dominant color of Thefacebook was blue. This was due to the fact that Zuckerberg has red-green color blindness, which he discovered after taking an online test. As he later said, "Blue is the richest color for me—I can see all of blue."[35]

Facebook's familiar blue color scheme was adopted because Zuckerberg's color blindness interferes with his perception of other colors, especially red and green.

Making It Fun

Five days after Thefacebook's launch, Zuckerberg was interviewed by the *Crimson*. He took the opportunity to point out features of his new site that he hoped would restore his reputation after the Facemash disaster. Zuckerberg said he built privacy rights into Thefacebook software. Users could only join if they had a Harvard e-mail address, and they had to use their real names. Users could set privacy options to determine who could see their information, specifying current students or just people in a user's class or residential house.

In interviews given at the time, Zuckerberg said he was careful not to publish any copyrighted material; that is, written words, music, or art created by a third party. He also said he was not trying to make money from the site. He promised not to sell e-mail addresses or other personal information to marketers. Zuckerberg mentioned that he considered making money by opening the Thefacebook to job hunters. Users would upload résumés, and the site would charge companies a fee for accessing Harvard job applicants. That idea was rejected, according to Zuckerberg, because "it would make everything more serious and less fun."[36]

Indeed, Thefacebook was about more than fun; it was also about vanity and competition, much like today's Facebook. Students uploaded their most flattering pictures, raced to gather the most friends, and bragged about their grades, their dating conquests, and other accomplishments. Perhaps this is what inspired about half of all Harvard undergraduates to open Thefacebook accounts the first week the site was online. By the end of February, three-quarters of all undergrads, around six thousand people, were using Thefacebook. The site was also used by a small number of graduate students and faculty members.

Thefacebook.com Craze

The popularity of the Thefacebook surprised even Zuckerberg. As news of the site spread to students at other colleges, Zuckerberg began receiving hundreds of e-mails from people requesting a version of Thefacebook for their own schools. Realizing he could not handle the work by himself, Zuckerberg promised Moskovitz 5 percent of the company if he helped expand the site to other campuses. Moskovitz dedicated himself to the task, working day and night to set up campus-specific Thefacebooks at Columbia, Stanford, and Yale by the end of February. Zuckerberg later praised Moskovitz for playing a critical role in the website's early days.

At Stanford alone, nearly three thousand students signed up the first week, and as at Harvard, people seemed addicted to the site. Shirin Sharif, editor of the *Stanford Daily*, described the attraction: "Classes are being skipped. Work is being ignored. Students are spending hours in front of their computers in utter fascination. Thefacebook.com craze has swept through campus."[37] Sharif interviewed Zuckerberg, who said Thefacebook was only costing him eighty-five dollars a month for hosting services, and he did not feel any urgency to make money from the site. As he told Sharif, "I know it sounds corny, but I'd love to improve people's lives, especially socially. . . . In the future we may sell ads to get the money back, but since providing the service is so cheap, we may choose to not do that for a while."[38]

By March 1 Thefacebook had more than ten thousand users nationwide, and other school newspapers were clamoring to interview the site's creator. But Zuckerberg was shy and disliked giving interviews, so he recruited his dorm roommate, Chris Hughes, to be Thefacebook's official spokesperson.

Something for the Long Term

In March, Moskovitz worked with Adam D'Angelo to open exclusive Thefacebook networks at Dartmouth, Cornell, Princeton, Brown, the University of Pennsylvania, Massachusetts Institute of Technology, and elsewhere. Although the Thefacebook users on one campus could not network with those on another, total membership soon grew to more than thirty thousand. This forced Zuckerberg to purchase space on five more servers at Manage.com, bringing his monthly costs to $450. And more servers

> "Classes are being skipped. Work is being ignored. Students are spending hours in front of their computers in utter fascination. Thefacebook.com craze has swept through campus."[37]
>
> —Shirin Sharif, editor of the *Stanford Daily*.

would soon be needed. To continue expanding Thefacebook's reach, Saverin and Zuckerberg, who used his college savings, invested $10,000 each in the company. To make back the money, Saverin began selling ads on the site in April. The first were from T-shirt companies, bars, and student moving services.

In mid-April, Saverin named himself Thefacebook's chief financial officer and officially incorporated the business as Thefacebook.com LLC. The partners were listed as Zuckerberg, Moskovitz, and Saverin, and they were soon fielding e-mails from major investors who wished to buy into the site, despite the fact that Zuckerberg still did not envision Thefacebook as a moneymaking venture. In June 2004 one financier offered Zuckerberg $10 million for the four-month-old site, which by now had 150,000 users on thirty campuses. Zuckerberg immediately turned him down. He later explained his logic: "I'm here to build something for the long term. Anything else is a distraction."[39]

As the site grew, Saverin was able to sell ads to large companies like MasterCard. Zuckerberg initially insisted that advertisers only be allowed to use small, bland banners designed by Thefacebook. For a time he also added a caption next to ads that read, "We don't like these [ads] either but they pay our bills."[40] However, Saverin eventually convinced Zuckerberg to allow advertisers to run larger ads.

A Plan to Dominate

Although Zuckerberg worked to keep Thefacebook running smoothly, he rarely signed on to the site and had little interest in the updates posted by his friends. This made Zuckerberg one of the Thefacebook's most unusual users. According to research by Moskovitz, some Thefacebook users were looking at hundreds of profiles a day, and a few were looking at thousands of profiles. This news gave Zuckerberg great confidence that Thefacebook was going to be successful. He was more interested in the site's popularity than its content. According to one friend, when discussing the site, Zuckerberg used the word *dominate* all the time. He planned to dominate the competition, and he was willing to work tirelessly until Thefacebook was the most popular social network in the world.

Chapter 3

The Trials and Triumphs of Building Facebook

In 2004 Thefacebook membership was growing rapidly. However, twenty-year-old Mark Zuckerberg was not convinced the site would remain popular forever, so he instituted a fallback plan. He spent hours creating Wirehog, a website where users could share music, video, and text files. And if Thefacebook remained popular, Zuckerberg planned to link it to Wirehog.

Zuckerberg first conceived of Wirehog at Harvard with fellow programmer Andrew McCollum. In June 2004 McCollum had a summer internship near Palo Alto, California, and he convinced Zuckerberg to rent a ranch house in the area to pass the summer. Palo Alto, home to Stanford University, is located in the middle of the region called Silicon Valley. Much of the research that led to the modern Internet was conducted in or around Palo Alto, and Silicon Valley was home to many high-tech companies, including Apple, Intel, and the video game maker Electronic Arts. Zuckerberg explained why he moved there for his summer break: "Palo Alto was kind of like this mythical place where all the [tech start-ups] used to come from. So I was like, I want to check that out."[41]

Let's Take Over the World

The four-bedroom Palo Alto house was home to Zuckerberg and McCollum as well as Zuckerberg's Harvard roommates Chris Hughes and Dustin Moskovitz. They were often joined by Sean Parker, who had met Zuckerberg a few months earlier in New York. Parker cofounded the music sharing site Napster in 1999 and made millions from its sale. He was very impressed with Zuckerberg's plans for Thefacebook. According to Parker, Zuckerberg was not planning a scheme to get rich quick. Instead, Zuckerberg told him, "Let's build something that has lasting cultural value and try to take over the world."[42]

Parker was a rising star in Silicon Valley. In 2002 he launched an online address book and social networking site called Plaxo, which worked with Microsoft's popular e-mail program Outlook. Plaxo quickly attracted 20 million users and was one of the first programs to go viral on the Internet. Parker was convinced that social networking was the way of the future and was an early investor in Friendster.

Like Zuckerberg's dorm room at Harvard, the Palo Alto house was cluttered with laptop computers, PCs, cables, modems, empty bottles and cans, food wrappers, and other trash. Zuckerberg often slept until noon and programmed late into the night, dressed in pajama bottoms and a T-shirt. There was little conversation, and when the men did need to communicate, they often did so through instant messaging. As the summer passed, Zuckerberg and Moskovitz kept Thefacebook running smoothly, fixing glitches, and setting up databases at several new schools.

The Undisputed Leader

While the coders spent their days staring at their laptops, Parker held meetings with Silicon Valley venture capital firms to determine their interest in Thefacebook. Venture capital companies provide financing for high-potential start-ups in exchange for a percentage of ownership. As Parker brought more recognition to Thefacebook, Zuckerberg named him president of the company. Parker moved into the Palo Alto house, bringing little more than his fancy BMW, which he allowed Zuckerberg and his friends to drive. (None of them had cars at the time; they walked everywhere.)

Thefacebook crew worked hard but also found time to party, using the website to invite mobs of Stanford students over to drink beer, watch movies, play video games, and swim in the backyard pool. Although marijuana

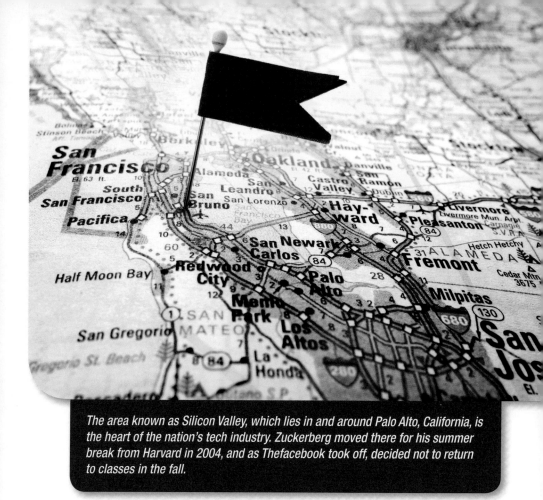

The area known as Silicon Valley, which lies in and around Palo Alto, California, is the heart of the nation's tech industry. Zuckerberg moved there for his summer break from Harvard in 2004, and as Thefacebook took off, decided not to return to classes in the fall.

was openly smoked at the house, Zuckerberg did not approve. According to Moskovitz, Zuckerberg was adamantly antidrug.

In August, as the beginning of the fall semester at Harvard drew near, Zuckerberg had little time to think about his college courses. Over the summer the number of Thefacebook users had doubled to around two hundred thousand. Rather than continue to run the site through Manage.com, Zuckerberg used money from the site's growing advertising revenue to set up his own servers in a warehouse about 12 miles (19 km) from Palo Alto. Thefacebook's expansion meant that the number of trips Zuckerberg took to the warehouse increased as more servers were regularly added. In addition to the cost of the servers, one of Thefacebook's largest expenses at the time was paying for electricity to power the networking equipment.

The Need for Speed

Zuckerberg was obsessed with keeping Thefacebook fast and glitch free. The rival site Friendster had quickly lost popularity due to its slow and overloaded servers, and Zuckerberg was determined not to make the same mistake. Every time there was an upgrade, Zuckerberg made sure he was adding enough server capacity so Thefacebook users would not have difficulties logging on to the site. As Zuckerberg told *Crimson* staff writer Kevin J. Feeney, "I need servers just as much as I need food. I could probably go a while without eating, but if we don't have enough servers then the site is screwed."[43]

Further pressure was added by Zuckerberg's plans to add seventy more campuses to Thefacebook's network by the fall. With a budding business to manage, Zuckerberg had no plans to return to school. He later said he "took about five minutes to decide"[44] that he would drop out of Harvard. Moskovitz decided to join him.

> "I need servers just as much as I need food. I could probably go a while without eating, but if we don't have enough servers then the [Thefacebook] site is screwed."[43]
>
> —Mark Zuckerberg, Facebook founder.

Borrowing a Little

In September 2004 the crew moved to a different rental house, and Thefacebook continued to expand its reach. The site was bringing in about $50,000 a month in ad revenue, and the company's five employees, including Zuckerberg, were collecting annual salaries of $65,000. Although Thefacebook was barely nine months old, it was one of the fastest-growing Internet start-ups in history. Many of Silicon Valley's biggest venture capital firms were taking notice.

Parker and Zuckerberg decided to make a deal with one investor they believed had the long-term vision to support Thefacebook. Peter Thiel was a founder of PayPal, the popular online payment site. In 2002, when PayPal was little more than two years old, Thiel sold it to eBay for $1.5 billion, pocketing $55 million on the deal. Thiel had also backed Friendster and LinkedIn, a business-oriented social network. Despite

Friendster's problems, Thiel remained convinced that social networks were an unstoppable trend.

Thiel agreed to meet with Zuckerberg and Parker to discuss Thefacebook. Rather than wear a suit and tie to this important meeting, Zuckerberg arrived in his usual attire: jeans, a T-shirt, and rubber Adidas flip-flops. Although Zuckerberg spoke little at the meeting, Thefacebook facts spoke for themselves; when a new school was added to the network, nearly the entire student body signed up within days, and 80 percent returned to the site daily. Thiel agreed to invest $500,000 in Thefacebook in exchange for a 10 percent stake in the company. Thiel believed it was a good investment, and he turned out to be right; when he sold his share in the company in 2012, his $500,000 stake was worth more than $1 billion.

Competition and Growth

Most of Thiel's money was used to buy servers. This allowed Thefacebook to expand to technical colleges and state schools. However, Thefacebook remained a small operation with a staff consisting of Zuckerberg, Moskovitz, Parker, Saverin, and a new hire, operations manager Taner Halicioglu. Together the crew managed to keep the site online as it grew to half a million users by October. Adding expensive new servers became a weekly activity.

Thefacebook was also facing competition from new social network sites. Myspace had more than 5 million users, and the site was very different from Thefacebook. Anyone could join Myspace; they did not have to be students at a particular college. Myspace was unconcerned about people using fake names and posting copyrighted material. In addition, copycat websites such as CollegeFacebook.com had gone online to siphon users from Thefacebook.

Despite the competition, Thefacebook hit 1 million users at the end of November 2004. The site was also pulling in more advertisers who were using what was then a unique strategy to attract customers. When Paramount wanted to advertise *The SpongeBob SquarePants Movie*, it set up

Broken and Burned

Mark Zuckerberg and five others who kept Thefacebook growing in the summer of 2004 lived and worked in a rented four-bedroom ranch house in Palo Alto, California. When not coding, the group threw wild parties at the house, open to any Thefacebook users at nearby Stanford University. Glass from broken bottles was swept into the backyard swimming pool, doors were broken off their hinges, and the chimney was damaged from a zip-line wire strung by Dustin Moskovitz. After four months, the owners of the house returned and discovered the damage Thefacebook crew had done to their home. In a court case, Zuckerberg was ordered to pay for the damages listed by the owners:

> The house appeared to be in total disarray and very dirty. Furniture out in garage—unsure about what is missing and/or broken. . . . Ashes from bar-b-q dumped—some on deck and some in a flowerpot out in back yard. Broken glass all around yard and some on deck. . . . An antique Indian basket . . . had been taken outside and left on top of the built-in bar-b-q. It was broken and burned.

Quoted in David Kirkpatrick, *The Facebook Effect*. New York: Simon & Schuster, 2010, p. 64.

a fan site on Thefacebook. Within days, more than 2,500 Thefacebook users mentioned the movie site. While the number is low, at the time it was considered a major breakthrough in viral marketing on a social network. Apple sponsored a similar site for fans of its products and offered discounts and free iTunes songs as part of its successful promotion.

Making a Deal

In February 2005 Thefacebook was available at 370 colleges, and the number of users hit 2 million. There were single days when more than 60,000 users joined Thefacebook, equaling a 3 percent growth rate in a 24-hour period. While Zuckerberg, Moskovitz, and the others worked around the clock to keep up with the website's skyrocketing popularity, Parker's cell phone rang almost nonstop. The viral progress of Thefacebook prompted a near hysterical response from investors eager to buy a piece of the site.

By March, twelve venture capital firms, four large technology companies, the corporation that owned the *Washington Post*, and the media company Viacom were making multimillion-dollar offers to partner with Thefacebook. Investors were aware that Thefacebook was bringing in revenue with its ads, but the company was not making a profit. However, one of the venture capital firms pursuing Thefacebook, Accel Partners, understood that the site could be very profitable in the future.

Accel executives understood that college students are what advertisers call a perfect target market. The term refers to a group of potential customers who are at an age when they form life-long buying habits, purchase their first cars, and apply for their first credit cards. Such customers often remained loyal to their early brand choices their entire lives. But advertisers also find it challenging to gain the attention of college students. Because they are busy studying, they watch little television and read fewer newspapers and magazines. Accel believed Thefacebook provided a perfect way to reach those elusive customers.

Accel employee Kevin Efrusy tried to reach Parker and Zuckerberg repeatedly, but his calls and e-mails were ignored. In his desperation to make a deal, Efrusy simply walked into the new offices of Thefacebook on Emerson Street in downtown Palo Alto. The walls of the office were spray-painted with multicolored graffiti, some of it obscene. Office furniture was being put together by the ten new employees Zuckerberg had hired, and half-empty beer bottles littered the space. Somehow, Efrusy made Zuckerberg and Parker an offer they could not refuse. In exchange for 10.7 percent of the company, Accel would provide $12.7 million to Thefacebook. Accel CEO Jim Breyer would add an extra $1 million of his own money. Because of its expected growth rate, the deal with Accel Partners put the value of Thefacebook at almost $98 million.

> "The dynamic of managing people and being CEO in a company is a lot different than being college roommates with someone."[45]
>
> —Mark Zuckerberg, Facebook founder.

Becoming a CEO

With the Accel investment, Thefacebook could hire new employees and buy more than enough servers to keep the site humming. But Zuckerberg, who celebrated his twenty-first birthday in May 2005, knew little about running a business. As Zuckerberg observed, "The dynamic of managing people and being CEO in a company is a lot different than being college roommates with someone."[45]

Despite the challenges, Zuckerberg worked hard and felt deeply responsible for Thefacebook's success. And unlike other Silicon Valley entrepreneurs who were known to have explosive temperaments, Zuckerberg got results without yelling and hurling insults at his employees. No matter how hectic or stressful the situation, he rarely showed anger.

Mark Zuckerberg poses with an oversized reproduction of the Facebook logo. By the time this photograph was taken in 2007, he had been CEO of the company for just under two years. He was not yet twenty-four years old.

However, in the new role as CEO overseeing a company with fifteen employees, Zuckerberg was forced to change some aspects of his behavior. He moved out of the rental house and found his own place, where he could live in a more ordered environment. He also stopped writing code so he could focus on company issues.

As Zuckerberg worked to turn Thefacebook into a real company, the site continued to flourish. The number of users jumped from 3 million in June 2005 to 5 million in October. By the end of the year, Thefacebook had invested $4.4 million in servers and networking equipment alone.

Turning Down a Billion

At the end of 2005, Thefacebook dropped "the" from its name and became simply Facebook. And the site continued on an upward trajectory with 7 million users. In June 2006 Facebook achieved a different sort of milestone; the Internet portal Yahoo! offered Zuckerberg $1 billion cash for his company. Facebook had recently turned down purchase offers from Myspace, NBC, and News Corp, which owns Fox News and the Fox Broadcasting Company. But the Yahoo! offer was the largest so far. Thiel said to Zuckerberg, "We should probably talk about this. A billion dollars is a lot of money."[46]

Thiel pointed out that Zuckerberg's share of the Yahoo! deal would be around $250 million. As usual, Zuckerberg did not seem impressed; he said he did not know what he would do with all that money except start another social network site like Facebook. However, after a few weeks of meetings with Thiel, Zuckerberg finally agreed to sell Facebook to Yahoo! And it seemed like a good deal; at the time Yahoo! had hundreds of millions of users who might join Facebook. However, days after the deal was announced, Yahoo! released financial figures showing that its sales and earning growth was slowing. The value of Yahoo! stock plunged 22 percent overnight, forcing the company CEO, Terry Semel, to cut the Facebook offer to $800 million. Two months later Semel once again offered $1 billion to buy Facebook, but by this time Zuckerberg had lost confidence in Yahoo! and rejected the offer. After the deal fell apart, *Wired* magazine wrote that Zuckerberg "became famous as the cocky youngster who turned down $1 billion."[47]

Feeding Controversy

In September 2006 Zuckerberg introduced a new Facebook feature called News Feed, which generated immediate controversy. If a user posted a status update, relationship change, or photograph, News Feed placed the information on their friends' pages in a streaming news format. Although Zuckerberg expected to receive widespread praise for the feature, some Facebook users were deeply unhappy because they felt News Feed violated their privacy. A Facebook group called Students Against Facebook News Feed attracted 258,000 members in less than a day. The group's mission statement claimed Facebook was stalking their every move. In part, it read, "You went a bit too far this time, Facebook. Very few of us want everyone automatically knowing what wc update. We want to feel just a LITTLE bit of privacy, even if it is Facebook. News Feed is just too creepy, too stalker-esque, and a feature that has to go."

Zuckerberg was totally unprepared for the controversy. The feature had an option that allowed users to remove any piece of data by clicking an X button next to it. Zuckerberg responded personally on the Facebook home page: "Calm down. Breathe. We hear you. We didn't take away any privacy options. None of your information is visible to anyone who couldn't see it before the changes." After the initial controversy, Facebook engineers worked day and night to build new privacy functions into News Feed.

Quoted in Kate Klonick, "Facebook 'Feeds' Online Privacy Debate," ABC News, September 8, 2006. http://abcnews.go.com.

Zuckerberg might have been arrogant, but he was also smart. In September 2006 Facebook membership was opened up to anyone in the world who was at least thirteen years old and had an e-mail address. This change in policy more than doubled Facebook membership to 12 million users. To keep up with the demands of the rapidly growing website, Zuckerberg went on a hiring binge, increasing the number of Facebook employees to 150. The workers were now spread out among three separate, overcrowded office buildings in downtown Palo Alto.

The expanding membership also drove the value of Facebook to nearly $6 billion. Zuckerberg's 25 percent share was worth $1.5 billion, making the twenty-three-year old Facebook CEO the richest man under twenty-five in the United States. He was also one of the most respected entrepreneurs in Silicon Valley and was often compared to tech visionaries like Apple's Steve Jobs and Microsoft's Bill Gates.

A Beacon for Ads

As his public profile grew, Zuckerberg searched for ways to put his personal stamp on Facebook. One of his ideas was a service called Beacon. It was launched in November 2007 to generate advertising dollars. Forty-four companies initially signed up with Beacon, which allowed them to access a user's Facebook page and gather information. In order to target their ads, Beacon advertisers collected information such as a person's likes and dislikes, activities, sexual orientation, and where he or she lived, worked, and went to school. In addition, if a person bought a product from a Beacon company's website, the purchase information would show up on the shopper's News Feed. It was hoped that customers' purchases would prompt their friends to buy products from the same website.

"Facebook must respect my privacy. They should not tell my friends what I buy on other sites—or let companies use my name to endorse their products—without my explicit permission."[48]

—MoveOn.org, a civil action group.

Beacon's purchase information appeared in shoppers' News Feed without their knowledge or permission. And it worked even if the shopper was not signed into Facebook at the time of purchase. This created considerable controversy. The civil action group MoveOn.org created an anti-Beacon Facebook group that attracted fifty thousand members within days. MoveOn.org circulated an online petition that read: "Facebook must respect my privacy. They should not tell my friends what I buy on other sites—or let companies use my name to endorse their products—without my explicit permission."[48]

Within a month, Zuckerberg was forced to issue another public apology. "We've made a lot of mistakes building this feature," he said, "but we've made even more with how we've handled them. We simply did a bad job with this release, and I apologize for it."[49] Zuckerberg attempted to fix Beacon by making it an opt-in service; users would only be on Beacon if they checked a box agreeing to the service's terms and conditions. Despite the change, MoveOn.org sued Facebook, along with companies such as Zappos.com, Overstock.com, and GameFly that participated in Beacon. As a result of the lawsuit, Facebook shut down Beacon.

The Winklevoss Lawsuit

The Beacon legal complaint was a minor problem compared with the lawsuit initiated in 2004 by Cameron Winklevoss, Tyler Winklevoss, and Divya Narendra. The three Harvard students had hired Zuckerberg in late 2003 to program their website, Harvard Connection. After doing about ten hours of work on the site, Zuckerberg quit, saying he wanted to concentrate on his own projects. Zuckerberg never had a contract with the Winklevoss group and was never paid the $400 they had promised him.

Harvard Connection was renamed ConnectU when it was launched in 2004. ConnectU was a dating website that offered coupons for bars and restaurants. However, Narendra and the Winklevosses claimed Zuckerberg stole their ideas and used them to launch Thefacebook. Although Thefacebook and ConnectU seem like entirely different concepts, the Winklevoss group sued Zuckerberg in federal court, and the case dragged on for years.

E-mail exchanges released during the course of the lawsuit show that Zuckerberg did not believe ConnectU would succeed. In an effort to cut his ties with the Winklevosses, Zuckerberg avoided them at school and did not answer their phone calls or e-mails. But six days after Thefacebook launched on February 4, 2004, Cameron Winklevoss left a message for Zuckerberg that accused him of stealing ConnectU's work and asking for an undisclosed sum of money.

A Harvard dean got involved in the dispute and asked Zuckerberg for his account of events. On February 17 Zuckerberg told the dean that the coding that had previously been done on ConnectU was already messy and bloated by the time he was hired. He stated that ConnectU would fail because the Winklevosses did not have enough servers, advertising, or original graphics for the site. In addition, he said none of his socially inept

Brothers Cameron and Tyler Winklevoss, shown here after a day in court, sued Mark Zuckerberg on the grounds that he had stolen ideas from their website ConnectU and used them to make Thefacebook successful. The case was settled out of court, and the settlement awarded the Winklevosses millions of dollars in cash and Facebook stock.

friends would be interested in the site. Zuckerberg told the dean, "I'm kind of appalled that they're threatening me after the work I've done for them. . . . I try to shrug it off as a minor annoyance that whenever I do something successful, every capitalist out there wants a piece of the action."[50]

Paying Out $65 Million

The Winklevosses were already very wealthy, which allowed them to hire a team of powerful lawyers to sue Zuckerberg in September 2004. The lawsuit accused Zuckerberg of stealing numerous Winklevoss ideas, including creating a social network for a college, providing a directory of people and their interests, providing a forum for the expression of opinions and ideas, and launching a site at Harvard with the intent of expanding it to other schools. Charges against Zuckerberg included copyright infringement, misappropriation of trade secrets, unjust enrichment, unfair business practices, fraud, and breach of confidence. The Winklevoss group asked to be granted ownership of Thefacebook and also to be paid damages equal to its value.

Observers of the case noted that Zuckerberg's creation was most likely influenced by Friendster, not ConnectU. However, by 2006, as the lawsuit *ConnectU LLC v. Mark Zuckerberg et al.* continued, Facebook was paying more than $20,000 a month in lawyer fees. In 2008 Zuckerberg wanted to put the lawsuit behind him and decided to settle. He agreed to pay the Winklevoss group $20 million in cash and 1.2 million shares of Facebook stock valued at $45 million. By this time the Winklevosses had pulled the plug on ConnectU, which was not attracting users or advertisers.

Even after the multimillion-dollar settlement, the Winklevosses were not happy. In 2010 they filed another lawsuit seeking further compensation. However, the appeals court rejected the second case in 2011. Presiding judge Alex Kozinski explained the decision, which summed up what many observers of the court battle believed from the beginning: "The Winklevosses are not the first parties bested by a competitor who then seek to gain through litigation what they were unable to achieve in the marketplace. At some point, litigation must come to an end. That point has now been reached."[51]

Redefining Social Networking

Although many companies embroiled in lawsuits find it difficult to attract investors who fear economic uncertainty, Facebook did not have that problem. In 2007 Microsoft invested $240 million in Facebook in exchange for 1.6 percent of the company. Facebook was now worth $15 billion, which pushed Zuckerberg's net worth to around $3.5 billion.

Facebook now had more than 50 million users. More than half were located outside the United States, which showed that the site had universal appeal. Although Facebook was little more than three years old and had yet to turn a profit, Zuckerberg's words from 2004 had come true. He built something of lasting cultural value, crushed competitors like Friendster and Myspace, and redefined the world of social networking.

Chapter 4

Connecting the World

In early 2009 Facebook had 360 million users worldwide. The company was on track to generate a total of $500 million from ads and was finally expected to turn a profit of around $10 million by year's end. Facebook had 850 employees working in ten separate offices in downtown Palo Alto.

On February 4, 2009, Facebook observed its fifth birthday, and Mark Zuckerberg celebrated by introducing a new feature, the Like button. This feature let users show they liked messages, photos, and other content posted by friends. The Like feature was an instant success and was clicked tens of thousands of times within the first hour. Commercial websites also loved the feature, and within a month more than one hundred thousand sites had added a Like on Facebook button to their own web pages. By 2010, according to Facebook chief operating officer (COO) Sheryl Sandberg, ten thousand websites were adding a Facebook Like button every day—equal to 3.65 million new websites per year.

> "The thing that I really care about is making the world more open and connected. . . . Open means having access to more information . . . And connected is helping people stay in touch and maintain empathy for each other."[52]
>
> —Mark Zuckerberg, Facebook founder.

In 2010, as Facebook's reach expanded into much of the online world, Zuckerberg was honored in much of the old media. *Time* named him Person of the Year, and Zuckerberg took the opportunity to explain his philosophy to readers of the magazine:

> The thing that I really care about is making the world more open and connected. . . . Open means having access to more information, right? More transparency, being able to share things and have a voice in the world. And connected is helping people stay in touch and maintain empathy for each other.[52]

Wiring a Revolution

Zuckerberg's desire to connect the world had unexpected consequences; in late 2010 Facebook helped unleash a political revolution. Events leading to the Arab Spring began in Egypt and spread to Tunisia and other Arab countries ruled by repressive dictators. The protestors were mostly young people connected to the Internet through their cell phones.

The political power of Facebook was first demonstrated in the summer of 2010 in Egypt when a young computer programmer named Khaled Said was dragged from a cybercafé in Alexandria by two plainclothes police officers who beat him to death in the street. Said was suspected of criticizing Egypt's dictatorial president, Hosni Mubarak, who had ruled the country for nearly thirty years. Said became a revolutionary icon when horrific photos of his corpse were posted to Facebook by his brother Ahmed. A Facebook group called We Are All Khaled eventually signed up 1.5 million members. Protesters used the photos to organize street demonstrations outside the police station near where Said was killed. Police brutally beat the activists, but videos and photos of the incident were uploaded to Facebook as well as Twitter and YouTube. Protests continued until Mubarak was overthrown in early 2011.

Facebook's Like feature, launched on the website's fifth anniversary, was an immediate hit with users and commercial websites alike. Within a month of the feature's debut, more than one hundred thousand websites had added Like us on Facebook buttons to their pages.

In December 2010 Facebook helped spark a revolution in Tunisia, where people banded together in demonstrations against the country's long-serving president, Zine El Abidine Ben Ali. Although Ben Ali had imposed strict Internet censorship, banning YouTube, Yahoo!, and other sites, around 2 million Tunisians had Facebook accounts. Among the Facebook users was a young man using the name Foetus who used the site to organize protests.

Foetus, who had ten thousand Facebook friends, posted grisly videos on the site of activists being killed by police in demonstrations throughout the country. Other videos showed grievously injured protesters dying of their wounds in a chaotic hospital setting. The images helped galvanize resistance, which resulted in Ben Ali's ouster in January 2011. Foetus credited the social networking site for playing a part: "Facebook is pretty much the GPS for this revolution. Without the street there's no revolution, but add Facebook to the street and you get real potential."[53] The Facebook photos and videos helped fuel protests across the Middle East. In the months that followed, the Arab Spring spread to Algeria, Jordon, Morocco, Kuwait, and elsewhere.

When the media credited Facebook for its role in the Arab Spring, Zuckerberg tried to downplay the idea. He said countless successful revolutions occurred before Facebook existed. However, in a letter later sent to investors, Zuckerberg seemed to have changed his attitude, saying he hoped to change the ways people related to their governments. He wrote:

By giving people the power to share, we are starting to see people make their voices heard on a different scale from what has historically been possible. These voices will increase in number and volume. They cannot be ignored. Over time, we expect governments will become more responsive to issues and concerns raised directly by all their people rather than through intermediaries controlled by a select few.[54]

Sheryl Sandberg

Mark Zuckerberg met Sheryl Sandberg at a Christmas party in 2007. Sandberg was a senior executive at Google who was responsible for building the company's profitable ad business. At the time, Zuckerberg was twenty-three and was still learning many aspects of the tech business. He was keenly interested in hearing what the thirty-eight-year-old Sandberg had to say, and the two talked for more than an hour.

Sandberg has a degree in economics from Harvard and made millions at Google, but she was seeking new opportunities. In early 2008 Zuckerberg was looking for a new COO for Facebook. In March 2008, after more than fifty hours of meetings, Zuckerberg felt comfortable enough with Sandberg to hire her as Facebook's COO. Once on board, Sandberg quickly meshed with Zuckerberg and the staff. She became the company's top salesperson and advertising champion. Because of her experience and input, Facebook showed its first profit in 2010.

Since taking on the high-profile job at Facebook, Sandberg has become a champion of women in business. Her 2013 best-selling book *Lean In: Women, Work, and the Will to Lead*, deals with issues such as lack of women in government and leadership positions.

The Giving Pledge

Closer to home, Zuckerberg was taking a personal role in addressing issues of poverty. In 2010 he signed on to a campaign called the Giving Pledge, which encourages the world's wealthiest people to give away at least 50 percent of their money to charitable causes. The Giving Pledge was initiated by Bill Gates and investor Warren Buffett and has been joined by more than ninety billionaires. After Zuckerberg committed to the cause, he called on other young entrepreneurs to follow suit, saying: "People wait until late in their career to give back. But why wait when there is so much to be done? With a generation of younger folks who have thrived on the success of their companies, there is a big opportunity for many of us to give back earlier in our lifetime and see the impact of our philanthropic efforts."[55]

Zuckerberg made another pledge in 2010 after meeting Cory Booker, mayor of Newark, New Jersey. Zuckerberg promised to provide $100 million for Booker's Startup: Education, a program founded to improve Newark's public schools. Appearing on *The Oprah Winfrey Show* flanked by Booker and New Jersey governor Chris Christie, Zuckerberg announced, "I've had a lot of opportunities in my life and a lot of that comes from having gone to really good schools. And I want to do what I can to make sure everyone has those opportunities."[56]

Zuckerberg had a great deal of money to give away. In 2011 *Forbes* released its list of American billionaires; Zuckerberg was number thirty-five, with an estimated net worth of $13.5 billion. Five other Facebook founders were on the list, including Dustin Moskovitz ($2.7 billion), Sean Parker ($1.6 billion), and Eduardo Saverin ($1.5 billion).

> "I've had a lot of opportunities in my life and a lot of that comes from having gone to really good schools. And I want to do what I can to make sure everyone has those opportunities."[56]
>
> —Mark Zuckerberg, Facebook founder.

A New Headquarters

Zuckerberg's fortunes grew along with Facebook. In 2011 the company had thirty-two hundred employees. Around two thousand were located in Palo Alto; the rest worked in twelve other locations across the United States and twenty-four small international offices in places such as Amsterdam, Netherlands; Seoul, South Korea; and Warsaw, Poland.

Facebook's profits had increased 87 percent over 2010, reaching $1 billion. Zuckerberg used some of that money to purchase a new corporate headquarters, the old Sun Microsystems site in the affluent city of Menlo Park, California, less than 3 miles (4.8 km) from Palo Alto. To honor his college code monkey days, Zuckerberg changed the name of the ring road around the site from Network Circle to Hacker Way.

The new Facebook headquarters consisted of ten buildings on a 1-million-square-foot (92,903 sq m) area. But even this massive property was not considered large enough to house Facebook because Zucker-

Facebook moved into this multibuilding complex in 2010. Despite the facility's enormous size, plans were immediately made to expand it to accommodate the thousands of new employees the company planned to hire.

berg planned to add thousands of new employees. Almost immediately, Facebook broke ground on a second site nearby, to be connected to the first by an underground tunnel.

Buying Instagram

In April 2012, as the new headquarters expanded, Zuckerberg made one of Facebook's first major acquisitions. The company bought the popular photo-sharing website Instagram for $1 billion. At the time, Instagram was one of the most downloaded applications for smartphones. Zuckerberg felt that the purchase would help Facebook gain a larger presence on mobile devices. He outlined his own reasons for the purchase on his

Move Fast and Break Things

Mark Zuckerberg spoke at the annual tech event TechCrunch Disrupt in San Francisco in 2013. In an interview, Zuckerberg explained the meaning of the Facebook motto "Move Fast and Break Things," which appears on posters hanging in company offices:

> I'm of the belief that values are only useful when they're controversial. There are companies that write all these value statements that I think are kind of meaningless because they're saying the same stuff. People are saying "be honest," and it's like, of course you're going to be honest. That's not a choice, that's a value, you have to be honest. Go home if you're not honest. Move fast is good because it's something that people passionately disagree with. . . . What I really mean by move fast is I want to empower people to try things out and I don't command that every [version] of what we release is perfect. What I optimize for is learning the most and having the best products 3, 5, 7 years from now.

Quoted in Justin Lafferty, "Mark Zuckerberg Reflects on IPO, Culture of Facebook at TechCrunch Disrupt," *Adweek*, September 11, 2013. www.adweek.com.

Facebook page: "For years, we've focused on building the best experience for sharing photos with your friends and family. Now, we'll be able to work even more closely with the Instagram team to also offer the best experiences for sharing beautiful mobile photos with people based on your interests."[57]

Financial analysts questioned the billion-dollar Instagram purchase, saying the company was worth only half a billion dollars. However, within two years Facebook was receiving more than half its revenue from smartphone customers. Analysts credited this change to the Instagram purchase, which exposed tens of millions of users to Facebook's advertisers.

Total Control and an IPO

Even as the Instagram purchase was making tech headlines, Zuckerberg was making plans to sell Facebook stock to the general public. This process is called an initial public offering, or IPO. With its IPO, Facebook would offer more than 421 million shares of company stock on the NASDAQ Stock Market for thirty-eight dollars a share.

The complex Facebook IPO was structured to give Zuckerberg 28 percent ownership but 57 percent control over the company's board of directors. This meant that Zuckerberg would be in complete control of Facebook, since a majority of stockholder votes is required to go forward with major decisions. This deal was quite unusual when compared to other corporations. For example, no entity owns more than 4.2 percent of America's largest company, ExxonMobil, and such entities are typically investment management firms, not individuals. According to financial reporter Matthew Yglesias, the structure of the IPO meant that "absolutely nothing—up to and including death—is going to dislodge Zuckerberg from control of his firm."[58]

Zuckerberg launched the Facebook IPO on May 18, 2012, from the Facebook headquarters in Menlo Park. Wearing his traditional hoodie, he rang the NASDAQ opening bell by remote control. Within thirty seconds investors had snapped up 82 million shares of Facebook. However, as trading continued, it appeared that investors thought Facebook shares were priced too high because the stock price did not rise as it had for other major tech offerings. Facebook stock started at $38 a share, briefly rose to $42, but ended the day at $38.23. Whatever the case, the IPO drove Facebook's value up to $81 billion, with Zuckerberg's share equal to around $22 billion.

> "Absolutely nothing—up to and including death—is going to dislodge Zuckerberg from control of his firm."[58]
>
> —Matthew Yglesias, financial reporter.

A Surprise Wedding

Two days after the IPO, Zuckerberg changed his Facebook status from "In a relationship" to "Married" after wedding his longtime girlfriend, Priscilla Chan. The couple had met at Harvard and dated off and on for nine years before tying the knot. Chan had recently completed graduate school at the University of California–San Francisco, where she earned a degree as a medical doctor specializing in pediatrics. For once, Zuckerberg took off his hoodie and put on a suit for the small, private ceremony held in the backyard of the couple's Palo Alto home. It was a surprise wedding. The one hundred guests thought they were invited to the Zuckerberg house to celebrate Chan's graduation.

Priscilla's work as a pediatrician inspired Zuckerberg to launch a new Facebook initiative fostering organ donations. The feature allows Facebook users to easily become organ donors by registering on the site and sharing their status as donors on their personal profiles. Zuckerberg explained the motivation for the initiative: "She's going to be a pediatrician so our dinner conversations are often about Facebook and ... the [sick] kids that she's meeting. She'll see them getting sicker and then all of a sudden an organ becomes available and she comes home and her face is all lit up because someone's life is going to [be] better because of this."[59]

Priscilla's medical work also influenced more Zuckerberg philanthropy. In 2015 the couple donated $75 million to San Francisco General Hospital, $25 million to the Centers for Disease Control and Prevention, and $5 million to Ravenswood Family Health Center, where Priscilla worked as a pediatrician.

Taking on Hard Problems

In May 2013 *Fortune* magazine released its annual ranking of the largest companies in the United States. Facebook made the Fortune 500 list of successful companies for the first time. With sixty-three hundred employees and a revenue of $5.1 billion, Facebook was listed at number 482. Just two companies on the list had CEOs who were under age forty; Zuckerberg was twenty-eight and Yahoo! CEO Marissa Mayer was thirty-seven.

In September, Zuckerberg appeared at Disrupt, an annual conference hosted by TechCrunch, an information technology website. Launched in 2011, Disrupt is an event where tech companies can demonstrate their newest products and services in front of venture capitalists, private investors, and the media. Prize money is awarded for the best ideas.

Zuckerberg was not at Disrupt to pitch new products. As one of the most successful hackers in history, he was a featured speaker. Zuckerberg told the tech crowd that although Facebook had 1 billion users, the number did not mean much to him:

> For a while . . . getting to a billion people was this big rallying cry. We started looking closer into it and it became apparent that it's not like we wake up and say, "OK, I want to get one-seventh of the world to do something.". . . But now, as we've approached that and passed that, the focus is retooling and retooling the company to go take on a lot of harder problems the world is facing.[60]

Zuckerberg felt one of the world's hardest problems was the lack of Internet access for people in developing countries. He said he was singularly focused on giving everyone in the world the tools to share whatever they wanted online. "That's been the unifying theme for us for as long as we've been around,"[61] he said.

Internet.org

To pursue the goal of worldwide Internet access, Zuckerberg partnered in 2013 with several mobile phone companies, including Samsung, Ericsson, and Nokia, to launch Internet.org. The goal of Internet.org is to bring affordable Internet to the 4.4 billion people on earth who lack online access. The companies pledged to work together to produce inexpensive, high-quality smartphones that would allow people to go online.

Zuckerberg's thoughts on Internet.org were contained in a ten-page paper he wrote called "Is Connectivity a Human Right?" In the paper, which he posted on Facebook, Zuckerberg points out that only one-third of the world's population has Internet access, or connectivity. He states that Internet adoption is only growing at 9 percent a year, and providing

Mark Zuckerberg arrives at an event intended to publicize Internet.org. The goal of the group is to promote Internet connectivity in developing countries, which its founders believe will benefit people in ways such as enabling them to find jobs and access health care.

worldwide connectivity is one of the greatest "challenges of our generation."[62] The need for access is not only to connect friends, families, and communities, but to provide a foundation for the global economy and promote social justice. Zuckerberg believes that by boosting connectivity, Internet.org can help people find jobs, start companies, challenge government policies, and access health care, education, and financial services.

The Connectivity Lab

One part of Internet.org is a project called the Connectivity Lab, which focuses on putting Internet hardware in place. About 80 percent of the world's population can access the Internet through their local cell phone networks. The other 20 percent, those who do not live in urban or semi-urban areas, have no such access. Many of these people live in the most remote places on earth.

Although satellites can be used to beam Internet access to the ground, they are extremely expensive to build and launch into space. Connectivity Lab hopes to remedy the situation by developing futuristic means to replace satellites. One such method would use a new generation of drones that could operate at high altitudes, 65,000 feet (19,812 m) above the earth. A single such drone, or unmanned aerial vehicle, could beam an Internet signal over a city-sized area of rural territory. The solar-powered drone would generate power from the sun during the day to store it in batteries for night use. Zuckerberg writes, "With the efficiency and endurance of high altitude drones, it's even possible that the aircraft could remain aloft for months or years. . . . And unlike satellites, drones won't burn up in the atmosphere when their mission is complete. Instead, they can be easily returned to Earth for maintenance and redeployment."[63]

Whatever systems are used, people in rural areas could connect to the Internet using relatively cheap modems that receive signals from the sky and broadcast Wi-Fi signals to their cell phones or other devices. A single such modem could be used by an entire community.

WhatsApp

While Zuckerberg is working to bring Internet access to those who lack it, he is also concentrating on expanding Facebook's reach. To do so, he had Facebook purchase the smartphone messaging app WhatsApp in February 2014. Although analysts consider WhatsApp to be clunky and ugly, it is very popular outside the United States. It is used by nearly 1 billion people located in Europe, India, the Middle East, and Asia, where cell phone providers charge people for each instant message they send. The use of WhatsApp is free.

Facebook paid approximately $19 billion for WhatsApp. Some financial analysts thought Zuckerberg paid way too much, but he did not

have to consult with anyone before buying WhatsApp. With his 57 percent control of Facebook's board of directors, Zuckerberg could follow
his motto "Move Fast and Break Things," or do not be afraid to make
mistakes as long as you are not losing opportunities. And Zuckerberg
did move fast; he made the decision to purchase WhatsApp in a matter of weeks. At a large company like Microsoft, which also considered buying WhatsApp, it could take more than a year of meetings with
board members, investors, lawyers, and bankers in order to execute
such a large transaction. But as tech blogger Felix Salmon explains,
Facebook will be more successful with Zuckerberg in complete com-
mand of the company:

> The WhatsApp acquisition is a statement by Zuckerberg that
> mobile [phone technology] matters more than money. He's right
> about that. Without mobile, it doesn't matter how much money
> Facebook has. If you're asking whether Zuckerberg paid too
> much for WhatsApp, you're asking the wrong question. Zucker-
> berg is sending a message, here, that Facebook will never stop
> in its attempt to dominate mobile—that no amount of money is
> too much.[64]

A New Communication Platform

If WhatsApp helped allow Facebook to dominate worldwide mobile networking, Zuckerberg's $2 billion purchase of Oculus VR in March 2014
was a step toward ruling the future. The *VR* in the Oculus name stands for
"virtual reality," and the company's main product was the Rift headset.
According to Zuckerberg:

> When you put it on, you enter a completely immersive computer-
> generated environment, like a game or a movie scene or a place
> far away. The incredible thing about the technology is that you
> feel like you're actually present in another place with other peo-
> ple. People who try it say it's different from anything they've ever

experienced in their lives. Oculus's mission is to enable you to experience the impossible.[65]

The Oculus Rift was created to provide a 3-D view of virtual reality to gamers, but Zuckerberg wanted to take the technology into new realms. He envisioned students and teachers all over the world interacting in virtual reality classrooms and goggle-wearing patients in rural areas consulting doctors face-to-face. And, most important, the technology would integrate with Facebook. According to Zuckerberg, "This is really a new communication platform. By feeling truly present, you can share unbounded spaces and experiences with the people in your life. Imagine sharing not just moments with your friends online, but entire experiences and adventures."[66]

A Human Endeavor

If Oculus technology was integrated into Facebook, it would help increase the number of visitors to the site—and the numbers are already astounding. In 2015 Facebook had nearly 1.4 billion users, with 890 million of them logging on every day. Five new profiles were created on Facebook every second. Every sixty seconds Facebook users shared 2.5 million pieces of content and posted 293,000 status updates. Every day more than 3 billion Likes were added. Facebook users uploaded about 136,000 photos every minute, or 350 million new photos every day. These were added to the 250 billion photographs already on the site.

For more than a decade, from the earliest days of Thefacebook, Zuckerberg has claimed that he is interested in connecting the world, not selling ads. Although this is probably true, Zuckerberg today employs around ninety-two hundred people, and hundreds of them work to make Facebook the biggest advertising platform on the planet. So, whereas users love to Like things and upload photos from their recent

> "If you're asking whether Zuckerberg paid too much for WhatsApp, you're asking the wrong question. Zuckerberg is sending a message, here, that Facebook will never stop in its attempt to dominate mobile."[64]
>
> —Felix Salmon, tech blogger.

vacations, advertisers love to use this information to target ads at every sixth person on earth.

But even as the advertisers generate $4 billion a year for Facebook, users can ignore the ads. Facebook remains a place to solve problems through crowdsourcing, promote political ideas, and share life's joys and sorrows with friends and relatives. What began as computer code in Mark Zuckerberg's dorm room has grown into an entirely human endeavor. Today Facebook encompasses a world community linked by the thoughts, dreams, and desires of its 1.4 billion users.

Source Notes

Introduction: The New Face of Tech

1. Lev Grossman, "Person of the Year 2010: Mark Zuckerberg," *Time*, December 15, 2010. http://content.time.com.
2. Grossman, "Person of the Year 2010."
3. Mark Zuckerberg, "Connectivity Lab," Facebook, March 27, 2014. www.facebook.com.

Chapter One: A Computer Prodigy

4. Quoted in David Kirkpatrick, *The Facebook Effect*. New York: Simon & Schuster, 2010, p. 21.
5. Quoted in Matthew Shaer, "The Zuckerbergs of Dobbs Ferry," *New York*, May 6, 2012. http://nymag.com.
6. Quoted in Shaer, "The Zuckerbergs of Dobbs Ferry."
7. Quoted in Beth J. Harpaz, "Dr. Zuckerberg Talks About His Son Mark's Upbringing," *Salon*, February 4, 2011. www.salon.com.
8. Quoted in Grossman, "Person of the Year 2010."
9. Quoted in Shaer, "The Zuckerbergs of Dobbs Ferry."
10. Quoted in Harpaz, "Dr. Zuckerberg Talks About His Son Mark's Upbringing."
11. Quoted in Jose Antonio Vargas, "The Face of Facebook," *New Yorker*, September 20, 2010. www.newyorker.com.
12. Quoted in Vargas, "The Face of Facebook."
13. Quoted in Vargas, "The Face of Facebook."
14. Quoted in Lucy D. Chen, "Stick to Coding, Zuckerberg!," *Harvard Crimson*, December 12, 2007. www.thecrimson.com.
15. Quoted in Chen, "Stick to Coding, Zuckerberg!"
16. Quoted in S.F. Brickman, "Not-So-Artificial Intelligence," *Harvard Crimson*, October 23, 2003. www.thecrimson.com.
17. Quoted in Brickman, "Not-So-Artificial Intelligence."
18. Kirkpatrick, *The Facebook Effect*, p. 20.
19. Kirkpatrick, *The Facebook Effect*, p. 20.

20. Quoted in John Cassidy, "Me Media," *New Yorker*, May 15, 2006. www.newyorker.com.

21. Quoted in Kaja Whitehouse, "Zuckerberg's Diversity-Conscious Sis Making Silicon Valley Mark," *New York Post*, August 13, 2014. http://nypost.com.

Chapter Two: From Facemash to Thefacebook

22. Quoted in Kirkpatrick, *The Facebook Effect*, p. 19.

23. Kirkpatrick, *The Facebook Effect*, p. 23.

24. Quoted in Bari M. Schwartz, "Hot or Not? Website Briefly Judges Looks," *Harvard Crimson*, November 4, 2003. www.thecrimson.com.

25. Quoted in Schwartz, "Hot or Not? Website Briefly Judges Looks."

26. *Crimson* Staff, "M*A*S*H," *Harvard Crimson*, November 6, 2003. www.thecrimson.com.

27. *Crimson* Staff, "M*A*S*H."

28. Quoted in *Crimson* Staff, "M*A*S*H."

29. Quoted in Kirkpatrick, *The Facebook Effect*, p. 26.

30. Quoted in Tomio Geron, "Mark Zuckerberg: Don't Just Start a Company, Do Something Fundamental," *Forbes*, October 20, 2012. www.forbes.com.

31. Quoted in Ellen McGirt, "Hacker. Dropout. CEO," *Fast Company*, May 1, 2007. www.fastcompany.com.

32. *Crimson* Staff, "Put Online a Happy Face: Electronic Facebook for the Entire College Should Be Both Helpful and Entertaining for All," *Harvard Crimson*, December 11, 2003. www.thecrimson.com.

33. *Crimson* Staff, "M*A*S*H."

34. Quoted in Ben Mezrich, *The Accidental Billionaires: The Founding of Facebook; A Tale of Sex, Money, Genius and Betrayal*. New York: Anchor, 2009, p. 95.

35. Quoted in Vargas, "The Face of Facebook."

36. Quoted in Alan J. Tabak, "Hundreds Register for New Facebook Website," *Harvard Crimson*, February 9, 2004. www.thecrimson.com.

37. Shirin Sharif, "All the Cool Kids Are Doing It," *Stanford Daily*, March 5, 2004. http://stanforddailyarchive.com.

38. Sharif, "All the Cool Kids Are Doing It."

39. Quoted in McGirt, "Hacker. Dropout. CEO."
40. Quoted in Kirkpatrick, *The Facebook Effect*, p. 43.

Chapter Three: The Trials and Triumphs of Building Facebook

41. Quoted in Kevin J. Feeney, "Business Casual," *Harvard Crimson*, February 24, 2005. www.thecrimson.com.
42. Quoted in Kirkpatrick, *The Facebook Effect*, p. 47.
43. Quoted in Feeney, "Business Casual."
44. Quoted in Anna Vital, "Entrepreneurs Who Dropped Out," Funders and Founders, March 25, 2014. http://fundersandfounders.com.
45. Quoted in John Greathouse, "Startup Tips from College Dropouts," Openview Labs, July 5, 2012. http://labs.openviewpartners.com.
46. Quoted in Heather Leonard, "The Day Facebook Turned Down $1 Billion," *Business Insider*, March 13, 2013. www.businessinsider.com.
47. Fred Vogelstein, "How Mark Zuckerberg Turned Facebook into the Web's Hottest Platform," *Wired*, September 6, 2007. http://archive.wired.com.
48. MoveOn.org, "Facebook Must Respect Privacy," November 7, 2007. http://civ.moveon.org.
49. Mark Zuckerberg, "Thoughts on Beacon," Facebook, December 5, 2007. www.facebook.com.
50. Kirkpatrick, *The Facebook Effect*, p. 188.
51. Quoted in Jessica Guynn and Carol Williams, "Court Upholds Winklevoss Twins' Facebook Deal from 2008," *Los Angeles Times*, April 12, 2011. http://articles.latimes.com.

Chapter Four: Connecting the World

52. Quoted in Grossman, "Person of the Year 2010."
53. Quoted in John Pollock, "Streetbook," *MIT Technology Review*, August 23, 2011. www.technologyreview.com.
54. Quoted in Adrian Chen, "Mark Zuckerberg Takes Credit for Populist Revolutions Now That Facebook's Gone Public," February 2, 2012. http://gawker.com.
55. Quoted in Luisa Kroll and Mike Isaac, "Facebook's Zuckerberg to Give Away Half His Fortune," *Forbes*, December 19, 2010. www.forbes.com.

56. Quoted in Ryan Mac, "Mark Zuckerberg Finds Giving Spirit, Donates $500 Million to Silicon Valley Community Foundation," *Forbes*, December 18, 2012. www.forbes.com.

57. Quoted in Jessica Guynn, "Facebook Buying Instagram for $1 Billion in Cash and Stock," *Los Angeles Times*, April 9, 2012. http://articles.latimes.com.

58. Matthew Yglesias, "All Hail, Emperor Zuckerberg," *Slate*, February 3, 2012. www.slate.com.

59. Quoted in Alyssa Newcomb and Dean Schabner, "Mark Zuckerberg Marries Priscilla Chan in Surprise Ceremony," ABC News, May 20, 2012. http://abcnews.go.com.

60. Quoted in Justin Lafferty, "Mark Zuckerberg Reflects on IPO, Culture of Facebook at TechCrunch Disrupt," *Adweek*, September 11, 2014. www.adweek.com.

61. Quoted in Lafferty, "Mark Zuckerberg Reflects on IPO, Culture of Facebook at TechCrunch Disrupt."

62. Mark Zuckerberg, "Is Connectivity a Human Right?," Facebook, August 2013. https://fbcdn-dragon-a.akamaihd.net.

63. Mark Zuckerberg, "Connecting the World from the Sky," Facebook, 2014. https://fbcdn-dragon-a.akamaihd.net.

64. Felix Salmon, "Facebook's Horrible, Stroke-of-Genius IPO," Reuters, February 20, 2014. http://blogs.reuters.com.

65. Mark Zuckerberg, "Oculus RV," Facebook, March 25, 2014. www.facebook.com.

66. Zuckerberg, "Oculus RV."

Important Events in the Life of Mark Zuckerberg

1984

Mark Elliot Zuckerberg is born on May 14 in Dobbs Ferry, New York.

1990

Six-year-old Zuckerberg learns to write computer code using Atari BASIC programming.

1996

Zuckerberg creates ZuckNet software that allows his family members to use their personal computers to send instant messages to each other.

2000

Zuckerberg enrolls in the prestigious Phillips Exeter Academy.

2002

Zuckerberg enrolls in Harvard University.

2003

Zuckerberg launches the controversial Facemash website, which allows Harvard student users to compare photos of their peers and vote on their looks.

2004

On February 4 Zuckerberg launches Thefacebook social networking site from his dorm room at Harvard. The site is initially open only to Harvard students, but in time Zuckerberg opens Thefacebook sites at other universities.

2005

Thefacebook drops "the" from its name, becoming simply Facebook.

2006

In September Facebook opens up membership to anyone in the world who is at least thirteen years old and has an e-mail address.

2007
Microsoft invests $240 million in Facebook in exchange for 1.6 percent of the company.

2008
Zuckerberg hires Sheryl Sandberg as Facebook's chief operating officer.

2009
The Ben Mezrich book *The Accidental Billionaires*, about Zuckerberg's early days at Harvard, is published. Director David Fincher's movie *The Social Network*, based on the book, is released the following year.

2010
Zuckerberg is named *Time* magazine's Person of the Year for connecting more than half a billion people through Facebook.

2011
In the *Forbes* ranking of American billionaires, Zuckerberg is number thirty-five, with an estimated net worth of $13.5 billion.

2012
In May Facebook holds an initial public offering, selling company stock on the NASDAQ Stock Market for thirty-eight dollars a share. Zuckerberg marries his longtime girlfriend, Priscilla Chan, two days later.

2013
Zuckerberg partners with several mobile phone companies to launch Internet.org with the goal of bringing affordable Internet to the 4.4 billion people on earth who lack online access.

2014
Zuckerberg purchases the popular messaging app WhatsApp for $19 billion to increase Facebook's share of the mobile phone advertising market.

2015
Facebook has nearly 1.4 billion monthly active users, around one out of every five people on earth.

For Further Research

Books

George Beahm, ed., *The Boy Billionaire: Mark Zuckerberg in His Own Words*. Evanston, IL: Agate B2, 2012.

Nikol Vega Canales, *All About Facebook and Mark Zuckerberg*. Seattle: Amazon Digital Services, 2014.

Daniel Gaetan-Beltran, ed., *Social Networking*. Farmington Hills, MI: Greenhaven, 2015.

Ben Mezrich, *The Accidental Billionaires: The Founding of Facebook; A Tale of Sex, Money, Genius and Betrayal*. New York: Anchor, 2009.

Carla Mooney, *Online Privacy and Social Media*. San Diego, CA: ReferencePoint, 2014.

Celicia Scott, *Facebook: How Mark Zuckerberg Connected More than a Billion Friends*. Broomall, PA: Mason Crest, 2014.

Monique Vescia, *Social Network-Powered Employment Opportunities*. New York: Rosen, 2014.

Internet Sources

Lev Grossman, "Person of the Year 2010: Mark Zuckerberg," *Time*, December 15, 2010. http://content.time.com/time/specials/packages/article/0,28804,2036683_2037183_2037185,00.html.

Jose Antonio Vargas, "The Face of Facebook," *New Yorker*, September 20, 2010. www.newyorker.com/magazine/2010/09/20/the-face-of-facebook.

Film

The Social Network. DVD. Directed by David Fincher. Culver City, CA: Columbia Pictures, 2010.

Websites

Facebook (www.facebook.com/facebook). Facebook has its own Facebook page, with photos, videos, a time line, and information about the social networking site.

Facebook Haters Unite! (http://facebookhaters.com). Although this site is slightly comical, it contains serious criticism and information about ways Facebook sells products and markets the personal information provided by users.

Internet.org (www.internet.org). This website is home to the Facebook partnership dedicated to bringing affordable Internet access to less-developed countries through Facebook's Connectivity Lab.

Mark Zuckerberg, Facebook (www.facebook.com/markzukerbergofficial). The Facebook page of the company's founder and CEO has a few personal photos, updates about various projects, and biographical information.

Picture Credits

About the Author

Stuart A. Kallen is the author of more than three hundred nonfiction books for children and young adults. He has written on topics ranging from the theory of relativity to the art of animation. In addition, Kallen has written award-winning children's videos and television scripts. In his spare time, he is a singer/songwriter/guitarist in San Diego.